P9-CCZ-134

For Nicole,
who possesses
"editorial superpowers."

Copyright © 2006 by Daniel San Souci.
All rights reserved. No part of this book may be reproduced in any form without the
written permission of the publisher, except in the case of brief quotations embodied in
critical articles or reviews.

Tricycle Press
an imprint of Ten Speed Press
P.O. Box 7123
Berkeley, California 94707
www.tricyclepress.com

Library of Congress Cataloging-in-Publication Data
San Souci, Daniel.
  The amazing ghost detectives / by Daniel San Souci.
    p. cm. -- (Clubhouse book)
  Summary: The boys enlist the aid of a neighborhood girl to track
down a ghost that keeps messing up the clubhouse.
  ISBN-13: 978-1-58246-165-6 ISBN-10: 1-58246-165-1
  [1. Ghosts--Fiction. 2. Clubs--Fiction.] I. Title. II. Series: San Souci,
Daniel. Clubhouse book.
  PZ7.S1946Am 2006
  [Fic]--dc22
                                                    2006005720

Design by Tasha Hall based on a
previous design by Toni Tajima and Daniel San Souci

Typeset in Stinky Butt

First Tricycle Press printing, 2006

Printed in Singapore

1 2 3 4 5 6 – 10 09 08 07 06

R0409419967

It all started one morning.

Someone had broken into the clubhouse and made a big mess. It was odd because the door was still locked and the window was shut from the inside.

"How did someone get the combination to our lock?" asked my older brother, Bobby.

No one had any idea.

Billy came up with a way to catch the mess maker. He tied some string to the clubhouse door and ran it across the backyard and into my brother's bedroom window.

He wrapped it around the trash can he had set on Bobby's desk and tied it in a knot.

"If anyone opens the clubhouse door, this can will hit the floor and wake you up," said Billy.

We all agreed he was a genius.

When Bobby awoke the next morning, the trash can was still on his desk.

But when we unlocked the clubhouse door, we found an even *bigger* mess.

"How can this happen?" asked Andy.

"I think I know," said Craig. "I bet it was a ghost. They can go right through walls."

"I don't think there's one around here," I said, shaking my head.

"Oh, yes there is," replied Craig. "That night when it was *so* windy, I heard a noise outside my bedroom window. When I looked, a ghost flew right by."

My younger brother, Mike, picked up some torn wrappers. "The ghost found our candy bars and ate them up," he said. "I didn't think they ate anything."

"We've got to get rid of that ghost," I said. "I'm tired of cleaning up the clubhouse!"

"But, how do we do that?" asked Billy. "We don't know a thing about ghosts."

"I know . . . I'll get Allison," said Bobby. "She did a big report on ghosts and got the best grade in the class. She lives just around the corner."

"Are you friends with her?" asked Billy.

"Well, sort of," said Bobby. "She asked me to help when she did her report."

In the afternoon, Bobby brought Allison to the clubhouse.

We found out that not only did she do that report, but her older sister read ghost stories all the time and told her everything!

"I *said* she was an expert," said Bobby.

Then we told her about the ghost in the neighborhood.

"Ghosts are serious business," she warned us. "They're hard to find and double hard to clear out."

"We'll do whatever we have to," I said. "We want that thing out of here!"

Allison agreed to help us.

We became "The Amazing Ghost Detectives,"

and made the clubhouse our headquarters.

We needed to know what we were up against, so it was my job to draw a picture of the ghost.

"What did you see out your window the other night?" I asked Craig.

"I don't remember much," he said. "It was kind of blurry and was flying fast."

But then Allison told me what she learned for her report and from her sister. Soon, everyone else jumped in and added something that they knew about ghosts.

When I finished the drawing, we all saw how horrible our ghost looked.

"Some ghosts are harmless," said Allison. "But I can tell this one isn't!"

"So if we find this ghost, what do we do?" asked Mike nervously.

"My sister says that in a lot of the ghost stories she reads, dogs can see ghosts and they're not afraid of them," said Allison. "When we find it, Molly can chase it away."

We all agreed this was a great idea and petted Molly for her bravery.

To track down the ghost, we needed clues. We split up and covered the neighborhood.

Bobby and Allison found that Mr. Turnipseed's bulldog Henry had barked for no reason on Monday.

Melissa and her sister Ashley showed Billy and Andy their sidewalk. Tuesday, it had been marked with mysterious signs.

Professor Stern told Mike and Craig that his television set had shut off by itself on Wednesday and smelled like burning rubber.

Mrs. Gray told Molly and me that she had found strange holes in all her flower beds on Thursday.

Back at the clubhouse, I drew a map of our block.

BOBBY'S   DANNY'S
           MIKE'S   ANDY'S   MRS. GRAY'S
                                             THURSDAY
                                             GHOST ATTACK

CLUBHOUSE

"Look! There's a pattern to where and when the ghost is making trouble," I said.

Sure enough, the ghost was on its way to Andy's house next.

"Oh no!" he moaned. "My parents are gone for a few days, and only my grandmother is staying with me."

We all agreed to meet at Andy's house after dinner. If the ghost showed up, we would be ready.

At Andy's house that evening, we could see that his grandmother was alone.

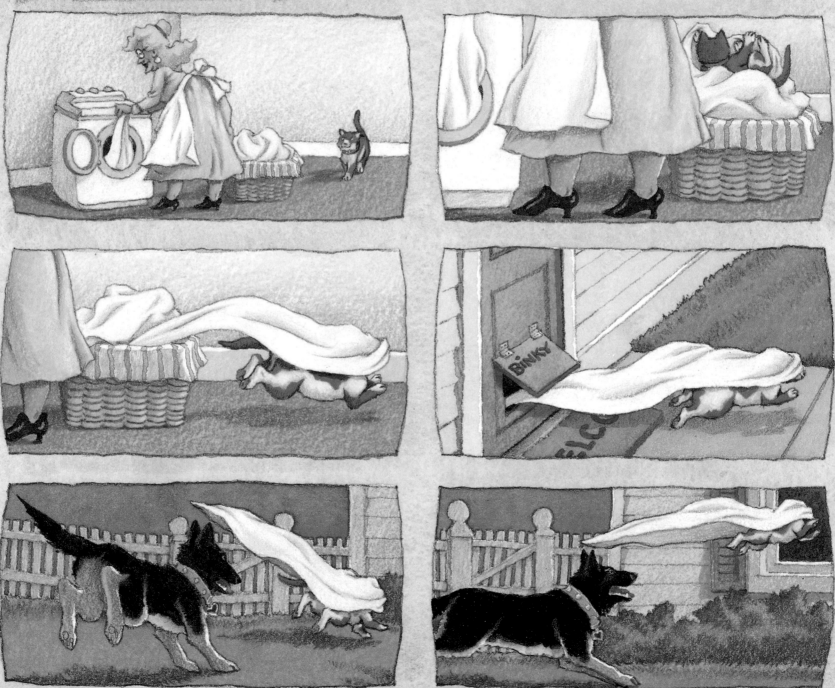

While we were looking for hiding places, Molly started barking.

"Look!" yelled Mike. "The ghost flew into the basement."
"What will my poor grandmother do?" cried Andy.

We climbed through the window and started searching for the ghost. It didn't take long to find it hiding in the shadows.

"It's after us!" yelled Allison. "Head for the stairs."
We raced up the stairs, burst into the kitchen pantry,
and slammed the door shut.

"I told you this ghost wasn't harmless," whispered Allison.
We listened for screams, but didn't hear any.

We cracked open the door and only saw Andy's grandmother. There was no trace of the ghost.

"Whew," sighed Andy. "We didn't catch the ghost this time, but at least my grandmother is okay."

But the good news didn't last long. Billy unfolded the map and said to my brothers and me, "Your house is next!"

We met at the clubhouse the next day to figure out how to get rid of the ghost.

"Maybe we could *scare* it away," Bobby said.

"That's it!" said Allison. "I read that there are places in the world where people paint their faces scary to chase ghosts away. We could do the same thing!"

We all agreed this was worth a try.

That night, we made our faces look terrifying with paint.
We put plastic horns on Molly.

then we hid outside our house and waited for the ghost to show up.

Suddenly, in the clubhouse, something crashed. Molly scrambled to the door and shoved it open.

She started barking loudly, but it was too dark for us to see.

She ran around inside, then raced back out the door.
"Molly's got the ghost on the run!" yelled Bobby.
Screaming and howling, we followed after brave Molly.

We chased the ghost down the street. We leaped over Mrs. Apple's hedge, hollering as we raced across her lawn. Lights went on and our neighbors came out to see what all the commotion was about.

"Hey!" shouted old Mr. Crenshaw. "Stop all that racket!"

But we didn't pay any attention to him. We kept following Molly, who was on the trail of the ghost.

Three blocks away we caught up with Molly. She had stopped barking. The ghost was nowhere in sight.

"Good job, Molly," I said, petting her.

"She turned out to be a great ghost chaser," said Allison.

Everyone took turns praising Molly for being so courageous. We were sure that we had chased the ghost right out of our neighborhood once and for all.

A week later, the ghost still hadn't returned so there was no more need for the Amazing Ghost Detectives.

Then, Arthur Gizeinski's mother found out he was allergic to bird feathers and made him give up all his homing pigeons. And that's how we became The Mighty Pigeon Club.